To Miles—
my forever sweet pea.
—AB

To to my darling, little
sweet peas.
—KC

ZONDERKIDZ

Little Sweet Pea, God Loves You
Copyright © 2019 by Zondervan
Illustrations © 2019 by Kit Chase
Written by Annette Bourland

This title is also available as a Zondervan ebook.

Requests for information should be addressed to:
Zonderkidz, 3900 *Sparks Drive SE, Grand Rapids, Michigan 49546*

ISBN 978-0-310-76699-5

Art direction and design: Cindy Davis

Printed in China

18 19 20 21 22 23 /DSC/ 22 21 20 19 18 17 16 15 14 13 12 11 10 9 8 7 6 5 4 3 2 1

Little Sweet Pea, God Loves You

illustrated by Kit Chase

ZONDERkidz

Little Sweet Pea, God loves you.
From button nose to gentle coo.

Squishy cheeks and sparkly eyes,
pure delight and perfect size.

Ears so dainty. Hair that swirls.
Around your neck are perfect curls.

You're God's creation, head to toe,
and he can't wait to watch you grow.

When you were born, God smiled with pride
then placed you gently by my side.

I kissed your face. I dried your tears.
God helped me to erase your fears.

Sweet Pea, I loved you from the start.
You changed my world and filled my heart.

I love your smell and smooth, soft skin;
the little dimple on your chin.

You're heaven-sent, a little star;
you're perfect just the way you are.

Sweet Pea, you were made for me.
You're right where you're supposed to be.

And when your little hand holds mine,
I know I'll love you for all time.

I see your smile and know your cry,
don't worry, Sweet Pea, I'm close by.

A tickle here, a tickle there—
you and me, we're quite a pair.

We sing,

we nap,

we laugh,

we play.

God watches over us each day.

But when I hum a simple tune,
you understand that bedtime's soon.

Back and forth we gently rock,
and in each other's arms we lock.

We'll snuggle up all through the night.
God's with us as I hold you tight.

I can't describe the love I feel
except to say it's oh, so real.

And joy deep down is mine to keep,
while you're awake or fast asleep.

Sweet child, you will forever be ...

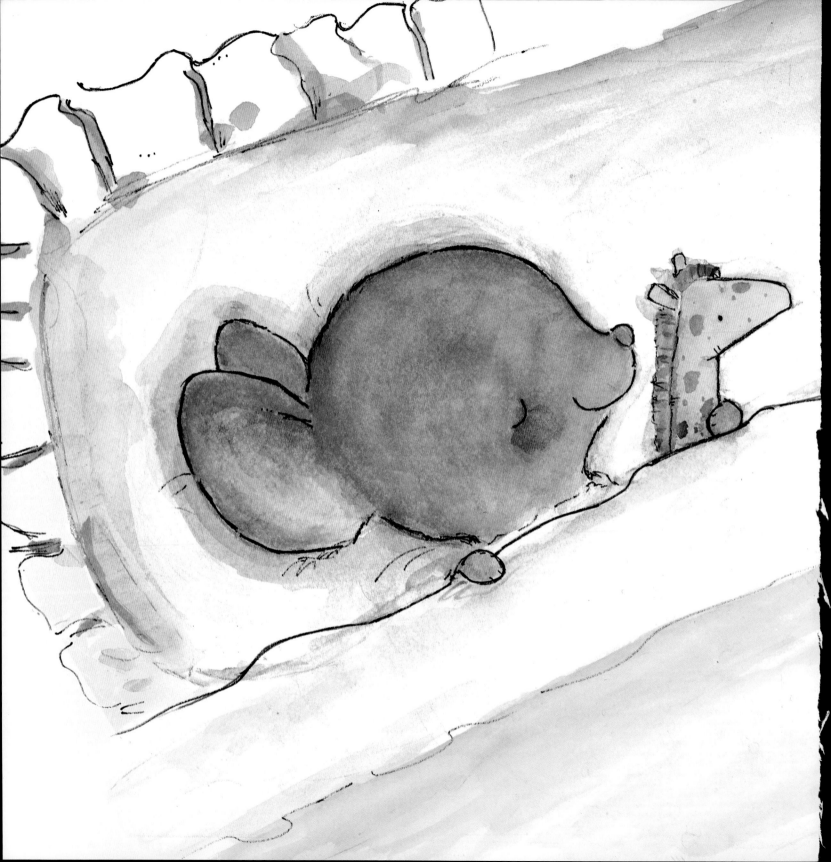

my heart, my love, my Little Sweet Pea.